This book belongs to

_____

LarryBoy in the Swim of Things

A Lesson in Being Generous

by
Thea Feldman

Illustrated by
Tom Bancroft and **Rob Corley**
Colored by Jon Conkling

SCHOLASTIC INC.

New York Toronto London Auckland Sydney
Mexico City New Delhi Hong Kong Buenos Aires

"Hi, Mayor Blueberry!" The Veggie Valley Elementary School swim team shouted and waved to the Mayor as she arrived at their practice.

"Why isn't Coach Artie Choke here yet?" asked Junior Asparagus.

"I'm afraid he isn't coming," the Mayor said. "It appears that he has won the lottery and flown to Fiji."

"Fiji!" said Laura. "But who's going to coach us?
We have a big swim meet coming up with Bumble
South Elementary."

"I know, it's a shame," said the Mayor. "This looks like
a job for—LarryBoy! I'll call and ask him immediately."

When the Mayor called, LarryBoy was immersed in a busy day. He was about to take a bath and was not too happy about being interrupted.

He was even less happy about coaching the swim team. "I have **other** important things to do," he told the Mayor, "like watching TV, eating pizza, and, oh yeah, catching bad guys."

"I promise this will take only a couple of hours a day,"
said the Mayor.
"And you could use the exercise, Master Larry,"
Alfred the butler chimed in.

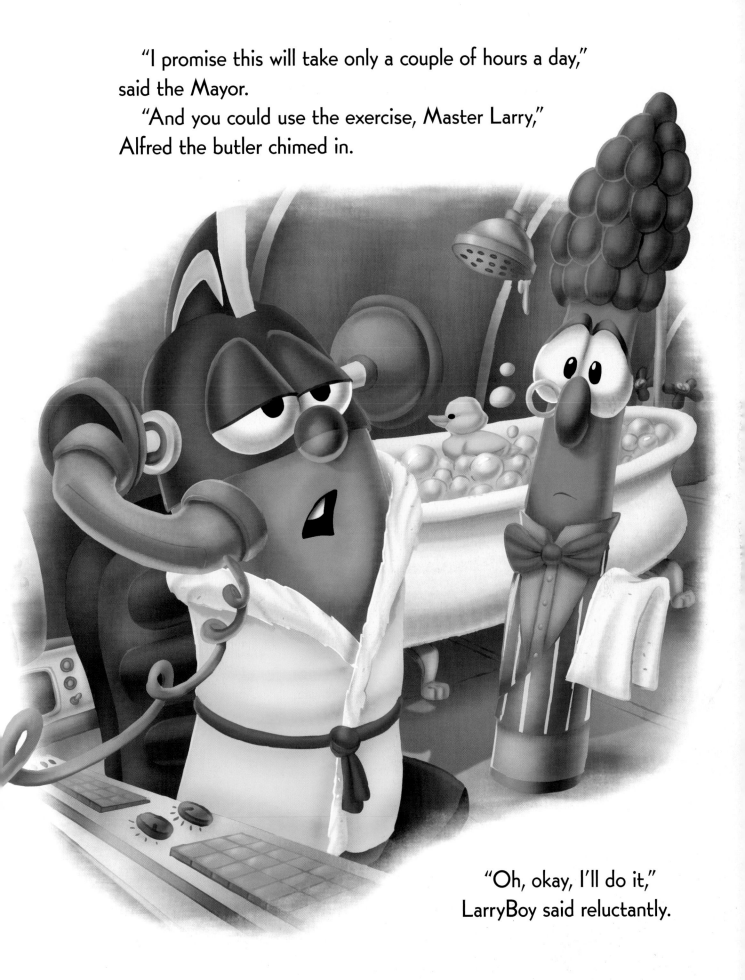

"Oh, okay, I'll do it,"
LarryBoy said reluctantly.

The next day, the team gathered at the pool to meet their new coach.

"This is going to be great," said Junior. "How can we possibly lose with LarryBoy as our coach?"

Everyone giggled and clapped excitedly.

The team waited for LarryBoy to arrive. They waited
and waited. Finally, the kids gave up.
"It looks like he isn't coming," Laura said sadly.
Everyone wilted with disappointment.

Just as practice time was about to end, LarryBoy
moseyed in, reading a newspaper and eating a donut.
Because he didn't so much as glance at the team, LarryBoy
missed their disappointed faces.

When LarryBoy finally put the paper down, he discovered that he was alone. "Well, that's a fine welcome," he said. "Here I am giving my time to this team, and they don't even show up."

"I'm getting pretty steamed," LarryBoy said. "I could be doing something more interesting than talking to myself by an empty pool!"

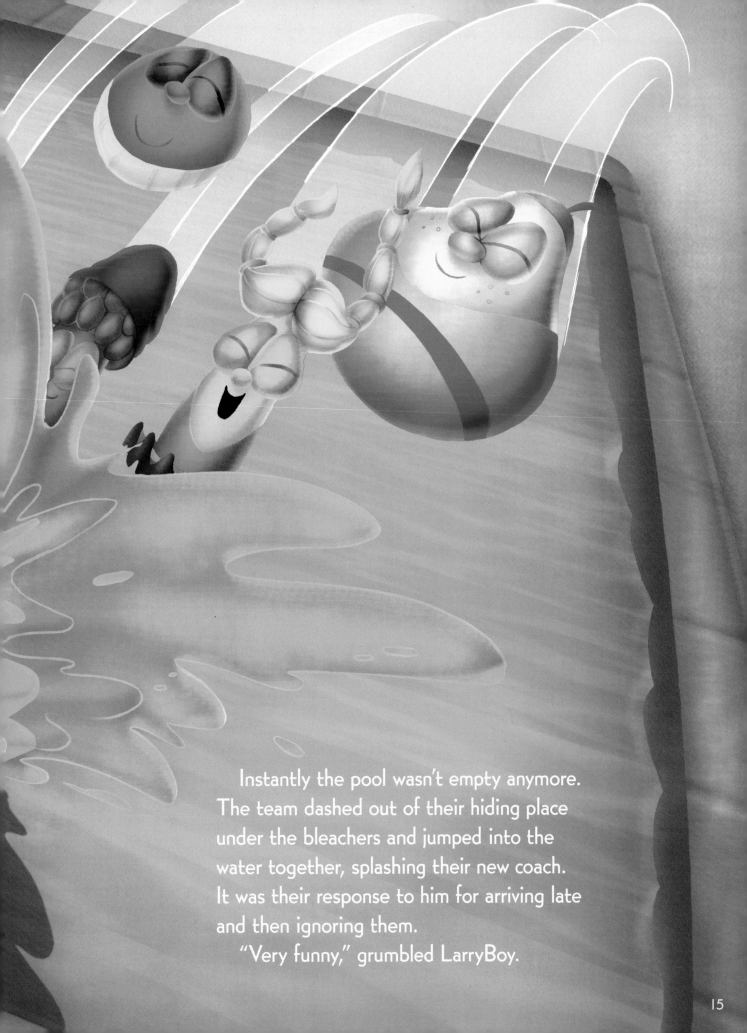

Instantly the pool wasn't empty anymore. The team dashed out of their hiding place under the bleachers and jumped into the water together, splashing their new coach. It was their response to him for arriving late and then ignoring them.

"Very funny," grumbled LarryBoy.

Things didn't get much better in the following days. LarryBoy managed to get to practice on time, but he left early every day. "See you tomorrow, kids. I have Plunger Practice," he would say and leave.

The team wanted LarryBoy's time and attention. And they were *not* getting it.

So the kids began to play pranks on LarryBoy. They replaced his whistle with a kazoo.

They swapped his striped swim cap with a floral shower cap.

And LarryBoy was always wet, even though he never went into the pool.

LarryBoy finally realized that things weren't going very well between him and the team. He also noticed how much the kids loved to swim. So one day, he arranged an obstacle course in the water and coached the team through it.

"Right, left, right, left—go, go, go!" shouted LarryBoy with excitement. "You're doing great! Keep this up and tomorrow I'll show you my famous plunger paddle stroke," he promised.

And he did. But the team wasn't ready to forgive their coach yet. The next day, all the kids skipped practice.

At the following practice, LarryBoy let them have it. "Do you know I could be waxing the Larrymobile or taking hula lessons instead of waiting around for you?" he shouted. "But more importantly, this is *your* time, *your* practice. Don't waste it!"

The team was stunned. LarryBoy really cared about them! That was all the kids needed to know.

Now, they were ready to work together with their coach.
And their coach was ready to work with his team.
    The team practices may not have been perfect, but
at least everyone was working hard. And Coach
LarryBoy even let them have some fun, too!

Then one day, LarryBoy returned home, checked his mail, and found an invitation waiting for him. "Alfred!" LarryBoy cried. "They're holding a banquet in my honor!"

"Too bad you can't go,
Master Larry," said Alfred.
"What do you mean?"
LarryBoy asked.
"It's the same night as the
swim meet against Bumble South
Elementary," Alfred reminded him.

"But Alfred, think of all the applause—for me; and a trophy—for me; and those cheesy puffs—a whole plate for me!" said LarryBoy, dreaming of his big night.

"But the team needs me, too," LarryBoy said in the next breath, thinking of how much he didn't want to disappoint the kids ever again.

LarryBoy knew there was only one thing to do—coach the team! Once he had made the decision, LarryBoy felt great, imagining the swim meet. "I have to spend that night with the kids. They've been working so hard!" he said.

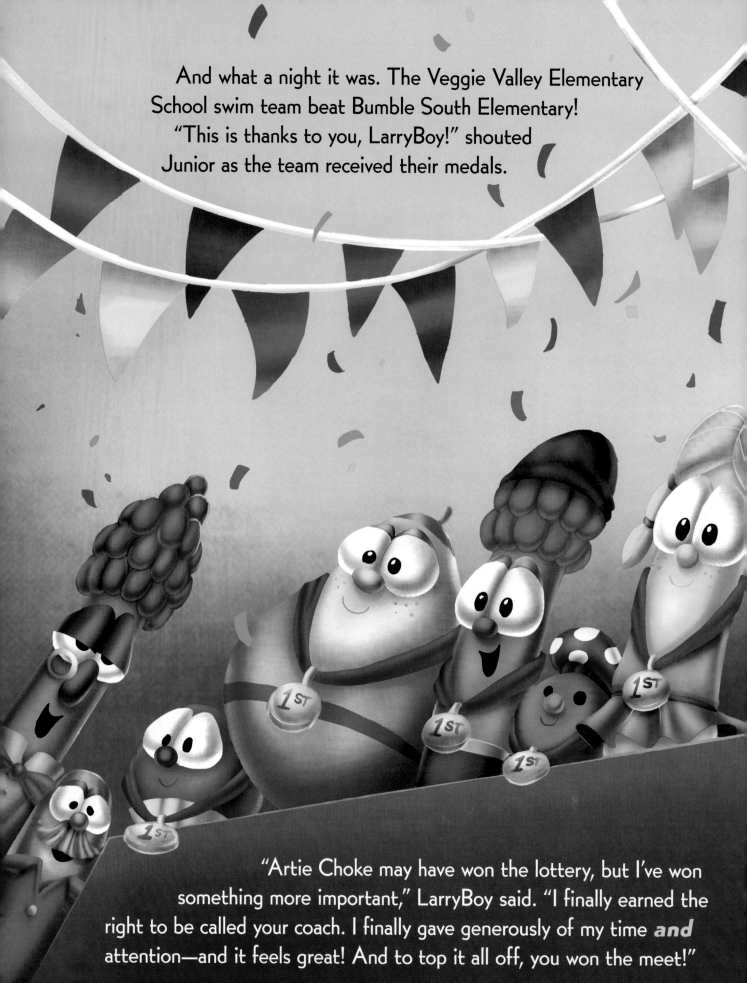

And what a night it was. The Veggie Valley Elementary
School swim team beat Bumble South Elementary!
"This is thanks to you, LarryBoy!" shouted
Junior as the team received their medals.

"Artie Choke may have won the lottery, but I've won
something more important," LarryBoy said. "I finally earned the
right to be called your coach. I finally gave generously of my time *and*
attention—and it feels great! And to top it all off, you won the meet!"

"**You** are a winner, too, LarryBoy!" said the Mayor as she handed him his Cucumber of the Year trophy from the banquet that he had missed. It was filled to the brim with his favorite snack.

"Last month, I might have wanted to keep the snacks all to myself," said LarryBoy. "But a good coach shares his time *and* his cheesy puffs!" he added, passing out handfuls to everyone.